Wonderfully Wacky

SCIENCE
RIDDLES

For Curious Kids

THE PUZZLE PATCH

What is now proved was once only imagined.

....

THANK YOU

AS AN INDEPENDENT PUBLISHER

We rely on you.

Please let us know if we can make your experience even better. We respect constructive criticism as it allows us to keep getting better. If you have any issues, message us online!

Please consider leaving us a review on Amazon!

Dear Parents,

We are excited to present "Wonderfully Wacky Science Riddles for Curious Kids." Each riddle in this collection has been carefully crafted to be entertaining and educational, sparking your imagination and providing valuable insights into the amazing world of science.

The book focuses on different areas of science, including space exploration, famous scientists and inventors, genetics, astronomy, animals, geology, energy, and more. Within each chapter, we have included ten riddles that will challenge and entertain your child.

You'll find that each category is carefully organized to make your experience both enjoyable and educational. Here's a breakdown of how the book works and some recommendations for making the most out of your riddle-solving adventure:

- Each category has 10 riddles and fun facts.
- Write down your answers before checking the answer key.
- Some concepts may be challenging; parent involvement is encouraged for discussion and explanation.
- These riddles aim to spark conversations and exploration, fostering a lifelong love of learning and discovery for kids and parents alike.

So, gather your family, grab a pen and paper, and embark on an exciting adventure filled with laughter, learning, and curiosity. With each riddle, you'll uncover new wonders and mysteries, and by working together, you'll create memories that will last a lifetime. Happy riddling!

Space Exploration and NASA

Space travel, NASA, and the study of the universe.

1. I'm a giant ball of gas burning bright, I'm at the center of your day and night. What am I?

2. I am a beautiful ringed wonder, the sixth planet from the Sun; which planet am I?

3. We've walked on my surface, and I'm Earth's closest neighbor. Who am I?

Space Exploration and NASA

4. I am the famous American spacecraft that took the first humans to the Moon.
What is my name?

5. I go up but never come down. What am I?

6. I am the red planet and the fourth from the Sun; who am I?

7. I'm a man-made home that orbits Earth, where astronauts live and work. What am I?

Space Exploration and NASA

Did You Know: NASA was established in 1958

8. I am Earth's twin sister in size but not in temperature.
Which planet am I?

9. I was the first human-made object to reach the Moon, sent by the USSR. What was my name?

10. I am the largest object in the asteroid belt and classified as a dwarf planet. Who am I?

Space Exploration and NASA

Fun Facts

The International Space Station is approximately the size of a football field and orbits Earth at an altitude of about 250 miles.

Mars has the largest volcano in our solar system, Olympus Mons, which is about 13.6 miles high.

Answer Key

1. The Sun
2. Saturn
3. The Moon
4. Apollo 11
5. A rocket
6. Mars
7. The Space Station
8. Venus
9. Luna 2
10. Ceres

Dinosaurs and Fossils:

Exploring prehistoric creatures and the study of fossils

1. I ruled the land with a fearsome roar, the king of dinosaurs you can't ignore. Who am I?

2. With a neck so long and legs so tall, I munched on leaves; no tree too tall. Who am I?

3. I had plates on my back and spikes on my tail, don't mess with me, or you'll be impaled! Who am I?

Dinosaurs and Fossils:

4. Fast as lightning, I would sprint; with three sharp claws, I left a print. Who am I?

5. I had wings like a bat, but I'm not one; I soared through the skies; it was so much fun! Who am I?

6. With horns on my head and a massive frame, I grazed the land, a herbivore's game. Who am I?

7. I'm not just dusty in the ground, I'm a story from long ago, waiting to be found. What am I?

Dinosaurs and Fossils:

Did You Know: There are 700 different species of dinosaurs discovered so far.

8. My tail was like a whip, and my name sounds like a dip, but I roamed the land without a ship. Who am I?

9. I'm a ferocious predator with a fishy name, but I lived on the land; hunting was my game. Who am I?

10. I was a bird-like dino, small and spry; my fossil showed feathers, no wings to fly. Who am I?

Dinosaurs and Fossils:

Fun Facts

The smallest dinosaur ever found is the Micro-raptor, about the size of a modern-day pigeon.

The largest dinosaur ever discovered is the Argentinosaurus, which could grow up to 100 feet long and weigh over 100 tons.

Answer Key

1. T-Rex
2. Brachiosaurus
3. Stegosaurus
4. Velociraptor
5. Pterodactyl
6. Triceratops
7. A fossil
8. Diplodocus
9. Spinosaurus
10. Archaeopteryx

Oceanography and Marine Life

Exploring the world's oceans
and animals.

1. I have no bones or brain, just tentacles to catch my prey in the ocean's terrain. Who am I?

2. I breathe through a hole on top of my head, I'm the largest animal, with a massive spread. Who am I?

3. With a shell on my back and flippers to glide, I'm slow on land, but in the sea, I take pride. Who am I?

Oceanography and Marine Life

4. I'm the king of the ocean, feared by all, with rows of teeth, I'm ready to brawl. Who am I?

5. I can change colors and shapes; it's true; blending in is what I do. Who am I?

6. I'm a mammal that lives in the sea with a playful spirit; watch me spin and flee. Who am I?

7. I live in the ocean, but I'm not a fish with five arms, I can grant your wish. Who am I?

Oceanography and Marine Life

Did You Know: The ocean covers more than 70% of the Earth's surface.

8. I'm the unicorn of the sea, my long spiraled tooth is a mystery. Who am I?

9. I'm a tiny light floating and glowing in the ocean's night; what a sight! Who am I?

10. I've got legs, lots of legs, and I crawl on the sea floor; I'm related to spiders, but I'm not one for sure. Who am I?

Oceanography and Marine Life

Fun Facts

The Great Barrier Reef in Australia is the largest living structure on Earth and can even be seen from space.

There are more than 200,000 identified marine species, and scientists estimate that there could be millions more.

Answer Key

1. Jellyfish
2. Blue Whale
3. Sea Turtle
4. Great White Shark
5. Octopus
6. Dolphin
7. Starfish
8. Narwhal
9. Bioluminescent plankton
10. Sea Spider

Famous Scientists and Inventors

Highlighting notable people who have made contributions to science and technology.

1. I loved to sit under trees, and when an apple fell, my mind did seize. Who am I, with gravity and motion expertise?

2. I had a bright idea one day; with a filament and some glass, I chased the night away. Who am I?

3. My hair was wild, my thoughts profound; I made time and space twist around. Who am I?

Famous Scientists and Inventors

4. I helped unravel a twisted ladder; the code of life was my subject matter. Who am I?

5. I peered through a tube, saw Jupiter's spots, and told the world my astronomical thoughts. Who am I?

6. I scratched a milkmaid's arm, and saved the world from smallpox charm. Who am I?

7. I glowed with pride as I studied rays, a woman of science, winning praise. Who am I?

Famous Scientists and Inventors

Did You Know: Albert Einstein was a passionate violin player.

8. I made great strides with pen and paper, writing books that took math lovers for rides.
Who am I?

9. I thought of machines that could compute, and during the war, I helped refute a secret code to boot. Who am I?

10. I soared above the clouds, a woman of flight, and ventured to space, breaking records at great heights. Who am I?

Famous Scientists and Inventors

Fun Facts

Thomas Edison was known as the "Wizard of Menlo Park" and was one of history's prolific inventors.

There are more than 200,000 identified marine species, and scientists estimate that there could be millions more.

Answer Key

1. Isaac Newton
2. Thomas Edison
3. Albert Einstein
4. James Watson
5. Galileo Galilei
6. Edward Jenner
7. Marie Curie
8. Alfred Whitehead
9. Alan Turing
10. Sally Ride

Genetics and heredity

Focused on the study of genes, inheritance, and DNA.

1. I'm the twisted ladder that holds life's key, with rungs of letters that make you unique. What am I?

2. I'm a set of instructions that make you who you are, found in every cell, like a microscopic memoir. What am I?

3. I come in pairs, one from mom and one from dad, I determine your traits, good and bad. What am I?

Genetics and heredity

4. I'm the study of how traits are passed through generations, a science that unravels life's fascinating equations. What am I?

5. I'm the father of genetics, with peas I played, discovering how traits are inherited and displayed. Who am I?

6. I can be dominant or recessive, it's true, and I determine if your eyes are brown or blue. What am I?

7. I'm the process that makes cells divide, with DNA copied and multiplied. What am I?

Genetics and heredity

Did You Know: The human genome contains over 3 billion DNA base pairs.

8. I'm the special cell division that makes gametes arise, with only half the chromosomes, for new life to materialize. What am I?

9. I'm a molecule that brings life's message, from DNA to proteins, I manage. What am I?

10. I'm a change in a gene, sometimes small, sometimes large, I can create new traits or an inherited charge. What am I?

Genetics and heredity

Fun Facts

Identical twins have almost the same DNA but are unique because genetics and environmental factors influence fingerprints during development.

A single gene determines some genetic traits, while others are influenced by multiple genes working together.

Answer Key

1. DNA
2. Genes
3. Chromosomes
4. Genetics
5. Gregor Mendel
6. An allele
7. Mitosis
8. Meiosis
9. RNA
10. Mutation

Zoology and Animals

Covering a wide variety of animals.

1. I'm a mammal who can fly in the night sky using sound to see. Who am I?

2. I'm a king of the jungle, with a mane so grand, my mighty roar can be heard across the land. Who am I?

3. I have a pouch for my young, hopping around under the sun. Who am I?

Zoology and Animals

4. I'm black and white and live in the cold, waddling around, I'm quite bold. Who am I?

5. I'm slow and steady, with a shell on my back, I carry my home, no need for a pack. Who am I?

6. I'm a tall spotted creature with a neck so high; I can reach the treetops and touch the sky. Who am I?

7. I'm small and busy, with wings that buzz; collecting nectar is what I love. Who am I?

Zoology and Animals

Did You Know: The smallest mammal in the world is the bumblebee bat.

8. I have eight legs and can spin a web, catching my prey; it's what I do best. Who am I?

9. I'm a striped hunter, swift and sly; in the grasslands, I sprint by. Who am I?

10. I'm a wise old bird, hooting through the night, with a head that turns, I'm quite a sight. Who am I?

Fun Facts

The blue whale is the largest animal on Earth, with a heart that weighs as much as a car and a tongue that weighs as much as an elephant.

The fastest land animal is the cheetah, which can run up to 70 miles per hour for short distances.

Answer Key

1. Bat
2. Lion
3. Kangaroo
4. Penguin
5. Tortoise
6. Giraffe
7. Bee
8. Spider
9. Cheetah
10. Owl

The Human Body

Focusing on the anatomy and physiology of the human body.

1. I'm the hardest substance in your body; I'm sturdy and steady. What am I?

2. I pump life through your veins with a beat and a rhythm, I keep you sustained. What am I?

3. I'm the body's largest organ, covering you head to toe, protecting you from harm and helping you grow. What am I?

The Human Body

4. I'm a pair of organs, like two sponges inside, taking in air so you can survive. What am I?

5. I help you stand tall and give you the strength to run and jump. What am I?

6. I'm like a computer in your head, with neatly spread thoughts and memories. What am I?

7. I'm a long, winding tube that breaks down your food from beginning to end; I'm here to do good. What am I?

The Human Body

8. I'm the windows to your soul, I let you see the world, in colors and shapes, a sight to behold.
What am I?

9. I come in pairs and help you hear the sounds of the world, both far and near. What am I?

10. I'm the liquid that flows through your veins, carrying oxygen and nutrients with every beat I sustain. What am I?

The Human Body

Answer Key

1. Tooth enamel
2. Heart
3. Skin
4. Lungs
5. Skeleton
6. Brain
7. Digestive system
8. Eyes
9. Ears
10. Blood

Geology and Earth Science
Exploring the study of rocks, minerals, and the Earth's physical structure.

1. I'm a natural disaster, shaking the ground, I can cause destruction when I'm around. What am I?

2. I'm a huge, slow-moving river of ice, carving the land, I change it precise. What am I?

3. I'm a hot liquid rock flowing from a volcano; when I cool down, new land I'll bestow. What am I?

Geology and Earth Science

4. I'm a shiny, precious stone found deep in the earth, I sparkle and gleam, revealing my worth.
What am I?

5. I'm a mighty mountain with a fiery top; I'll spew and pop when I'm angry. What am I?

6. I'm a process that makes the earth shake, with tectonic plates moving, a new landscape I'll make. What am I?

7. I'm the air layer surrounding the earth, keeping us warm and giving us mirth. What am I?

Geology and Earth Science

8. I'm a scientist studying rocks and the earth, uncovering mysteries and revealing their worth.
What am I?

9. I'm a rock that once was hot and liquid; now I'm cooled and solid; my story is vivid. What am I?

10. I fall from the sky and am vital for life; without me, there'd be nothing but strife. What am I?

Geology and Earth Science

Fun Facts

Mount Everest, the highest mountain on Earth, grows about 0.2 inches taller each year due to the movement of tectonic plates.

The Earth is around 4.6 billion years old, and the oldest rocks found on Earth are about 4 billion years old.

Answer Key

1. Earthquake
2. Glacier
3. Lava
4. Gemstone
5. Volcano
6. Plate tectonics
7. Atmosphere
8. Geologist
9. Igneous rock
10. Rain

Energy and Renewable Resources

Exploring the study of rocks, minerals, and the Earth's physical structure.

1. I'm a powerful force, blowing through the air, turning turbines, and creating power with flair.
What am I?

2. I rise in the east and set in the west, with rays that can power your home and the rest.
What am I?

3. I'm a power source always flowing, turning turbines with water that keeps going.
What am I?

Energy and Renewable Resources

4. I'm a heat source beneath the earth's crust; with steam and hot water, my power won't rust. What am I?

5. I'm made from plants and organic waste, providing fuel for vehicles and homes, don't let me go to waste! What am I?

6. I'm a method to power your home with no fuss, harness the sun, and leave the work to us. What am I?

7. I'm a type of energy, green and clean, derived from resources that won't deplete, a sustainable dream. What am I?

Energy and Renewable Resources

8. I'm a tall structure with blades that spin, capturing the wind and helping the environment win.
What am I?

9. I'm the power created by splitting an atom with tremendous energy and caution.
What am I?

10. I'm a way to save energy with a twist, a bulb that lasts longer and helps you persist.
What am I?

Energy and Renewable Resources

Fun Facts

In 2020, renewable energy sources accounted for around 11.6% of U.S. energy consumption and about 20% of electricity generation.

Renewable energy sources, like wind, solar, and hydroelectric power, are environmentally friendly alternatives to fossil fuels.

Answer Key

1. Wind
2. Sun
3. Hydroelectric power
4. Geothermal energy
5. Biofuel
6. Solar panels
7. Renewable energy
8. Wind Turbine
9. Nuclear energy
10. LED bulb

Science Experiments and Discoveries

Highlighting important scientific experiments and discoveries throughout history.

1. I'm the invisible force that keeps you on the ground; without me, you'd float around. What am I?

2. I'm a tiny building block that makes up everything, from the smallest ant to the tallest king. What am I?

3. I'm a paper that shows colors true; when you dip me in a liquid, I'll tell you its hue. What am I?

Science Experiments and Discoveries

4. I'm a gas that makes balloons rise high, and when you breathe me in, your voice sounds so spry. What am I?

5. I'm a powerful force, I can attract or repel with a push or a pull. What am I?

6. I'm a small piece of glass that helps you see through a microscope or telescope, I let you observe with glee. What am I?

7. I'm a substance that changes from a solid to a gas; skipping the liquid phase, I'm known to surpass. What am I?

Science Experiments and Discoveries

○ **Did You Know:** Isaac Newton, a famous scientist, discovered gravity.

8. I'm the process plants use to make food; I create a good mood with sunlight and water.
What am I?

9. I'm a fun experiment, mixing two things with a fizz and a bang, I'm like a science endeavor.
What am I?

10. I'm a shiny surface that reflects light, making rainbows appear, I'm a beautiful sight.
What am I?

Science Experiments and Discoveries

Fun Facts

The largest known living organism is the honey mushroom, which can cover an area of up to 3.7 square miles.

Rainbows are formed when sunlight is refracted, or bent, as it passes through water droplets in the air, splitting the light into its various colors.

Answer Key

1. Gravity
2. Atom
3. Litmus paper
4. Helium
5. Magnetism
6. Lens
7. Dry ice
8. Photosynthesis
9. Baking soda & vinegar reaction
10. Prism

Weather and Climate

A category of science that focuses on the study of atmospheric conditions

1. I'm a fluffy white shape up in the sky, with different forms, I change as I fly. What am I?

2. I'm a bright flash, followed by a loud boom; I light up the sky on a dark afternoon. What am I?

3. I'm a swirling, spinning wind, causing destruction wherever I've been. What am I?

Weather and Climate

4. I'm a chilly white blanket, covering the ground, kids love to play in me when I'm around. What am I?

5. I'm a collection of raindrops, frozen in flight, falling gently from the sky, I'm a beautiful sight. What am I?

6. I'm a colorful arc that appears after rain, with red, orange, yellow, green, blue, indigo, and violet, I'm a cheerful gain. What am I?

7. I'm the layer that protects the earth from harmful rays; without me, there'd be no sunny days. What am I?

Weather and Climate

8. I'm a cold, white ball, made from the sky's fall; when thrown at a friend, I bring laughter and joy, a delight to all. What am I?

9. I'm a small droplet of water that falls from the sky; when many of me gather, the ground will be spry. What am I?

10. I'm the temperature at which water turns to ice; I'm the point at which cold air feels not so nice. What am I?

Weather and Climate

Fun Facts

Lightning is a giant spark of electricity that occurs during a thunderstorm, while thunder is the sound created by the rapid expansion of air around the lightning bolt.

Clouds are made of tiny water droplets or ice crystals combined in the air and come in various shapes and sizes.

Answer Key

1. Cloud
2. Lightning and thunder
3. Tornado
4. Snow
5. Snowflake
6. Rainbow
7. Ozone layer
8. Snowball
9. Raindrop
10. Freezing point (32°F or 0°C)

Forces and Motion

The study of how objects move and the forces that cause them to move.

1. I'm the force that slows you down, making things stop when you slide on the ground or a spinning top. What am I?

2. I'm a force that makes objects stick, attracting them together and click. What am I?

3. I'm the push or the pull that makes things move, I can be strong or gentle, depending on my groove. What am I?

Forces and Motion

4. I'm a simple device, helping you lift things so nice: give me a pull and watch me work.
What am I?

5. I'm a force that pulls you down toward the earth's center; without me, you'd float around like an untethered inventor.
What am I?

6. I'm a wheel with a rope, helping to lift heavy loads, making work easier; it's me you should know.
What am I?

7. I'm the change in position or place of an object, making it go from one spot to another, I'm quite the subject. What am I?

Forces and Motion

8. I'm a sloping surface that makes moving things easier, from rolling barrels to sliding boxes, I'm a real pleaser. What am I?

9. I'm a force that acts on an object in motion, pushing it through the air, I can slow things down, so be aware. What am I?

10. I measure how fast an object moves; with speed and direction, I'm a key factor that improves. What am I?

Forces and Motion

Fun Facts

Friction is a force that opposes motion between two surfaces touching each other. It can be useful, like helping you grip objects or stop a car, but it can also cause unwanted heat or wear on materials.

Magnetism is a force that attracts certain materials, like iron, nickel, and cobalt, and can also cause objects to repel one another if their magnetic poles are aligned.

Answer Key

1. Friction
2. Magnetism
3. Force
4. Lever
5. Gravity

6. Pulley
7. Motion
8. Inclined plane
9. Air resistance
10. Velocity

Artificial Intelligence
Focused on the development and use of computer systems that can perform tasks.

1. I'm a machine that can learn and think with algorithms and data; I'm the missing link. What am I?

2. I'm a device that answers your questions with ease, with a built-in voice I aim to please.
What am I?

3. I'm an AI that mimics human thought, with deep learning and neural nets I've been taught.
What am I?

Artificial Intelligence

4. I'm a program that helps you find your way; with maps and directions, I guide your day. What am I?

5. I'm a robot that sweeps up your floor; with sensors and AI, I clean even more. What am I?

6. I'm a famous test that measures AI's wit; if I can't tell it's a machine, it's a clever hit. What am I?

7. I'm a machine that learns from its mistakes, improving its skills; it's the future it takes. What am I?

Artificial Intelligence

Did You Know: "Artificial Intelligence" was first coined by John McCarthy in 1956.

---

8. I'm an AI that uses data to find patterns; with decision trees and rules, I help you solve matters. What am I?

---

9. I'm a clever machine that matches with humans and beats them too; from chess to Go, What am I?

---

10. I'm a digital network that connects things, from smart homes to self-driving cars, I'm the future. What am I?

Artificial Intelligence

Fun Facts

"Machine learning" is an AI that allows computers to learn from data and improve over time.

Did you know that AI can help doctors diagnose diseases and recommend treatments.

Answer Key

1. AI
2. Voice assistant
3. Neural Network
4. GPS navigation
5. Robotic vacuum
6. Turing Test
7. Machine learning algorithm
8. Expert system
9. AI gamer
10. Internet of Things

Periodic Table of Elements
Exploring the properties and behavior of different elements

1. I'm an element that's light and strong, used in airplanes and bikes, I help you get along.
   What am I?

2. I'm a noble gas that makes your voice sound high; you'll laugh and sigh when you breathe me in.
   What am I?

3. I'm a yellow element that's soft and shiny; people love to wear me as I'm quite fancy.
   What am I?

Periodic Table of Elements

4. I'm an essential element for life, I help you grow strong, keeping bones healthy and bright.
What am I?

5. I'm a liquid metal that's toxic and quick, I was once used in thermometers, but now I'm not the pick. What am I?

6. I'm an element that attracts to magnets with ease, used in construction and cars, I'm a popular squeeze. What am I?

7. I'm a light gas that makes balloons float, I'm essential for life, and that's no joke.
What am I?

Periodic Table of Elements

Did You Know: There are currently 118 known elements on the periodic table.

8. I'm an element essential for your breath; in the air we breathe, I'm the one that's left. What am I?

9. I'm a shiny, silver metal that's a good conductor used in wires and electronics; I'm quite the instructor. What am I?

10. I'm a non-metal element that's essential for life, I help plants grow strong and green, avoiding strife. What am I?

Periodic Table of Elements

Fun Facts

The heaviest naturally occurring element is uranium (U), with an atomic number of 92.

Hydrogen (H) is the universe's lightest and most abundant element.

Russian chemist Dmitri Mendeleev created the first periodic table in 1869.

Answer Key

1. Aluminum (Al)
2. Helium (He)
3. Gold (Au)
4. Calcium (Ca)
5. Mercury (Hg)
6. Iron (Fe)
7. Hydrogen (H)
8. Oxygen (O)
9. Copper (Cu)
10. Carbon (C)

Meteorology

Focusing on the study of atmospheric phenomena and weather patterns.

1. I'm a device that measures how fast the wind blows, helping meteorologists everyone knows. What am I?

2. I'm a scientist who studies the weather and climate, predicting rain, snow, and sunshine, I'm never late. What am I?

3. I'm a picture that shows patterns and data, helping you plan your day. What am I?

Meteorology

4. I'm a device that measures the air's wetness, telling you if it's humid or dry, I'm quite the witness. What am I?

5. I'm a large storm with a calm center, bringing strong winds and rain, I'm a weather inventor. What am I?

6. I'm a small, spinning vortex of air, often seen in the desert, I can be quite rare. What am I?

7. I'm a powerful, cold wind that blows from the poles, I can bring freezing temperatures; bundling up is my goal. What am I?

Meteorology

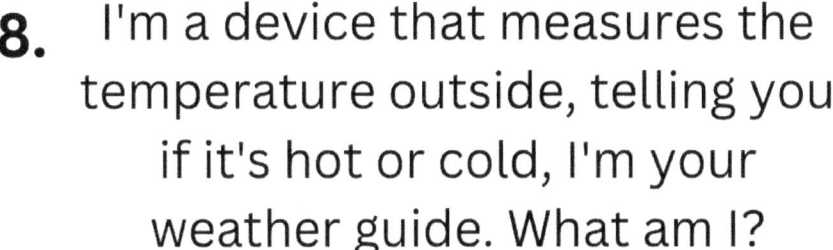

8. I'm a device that measures the temperature outside, telling you if it's hot or cold, I'm your weather guide. What am I?

9. I'm the line where the sky meets the land, watching the sun rise and set, I'm quite grand. What am I?

10. I'm a frozen ball that falls from the sky, often during a thunderstorm, watch out, I might drop by. What am I?

Meteorology

Fun Facts

The lowest temperature ever recorded on Earth was -89.2°C (-128.6°F) at the Soviet Union's Vostok Station in Antarctica.

Commonwealth Bay, Antarctica is the world's windiest place, with average wind speeds of 150 mph.

Answer Key

1. Anemometer
2. Meteorologist
3. Weather map
4. Hygrometer
5. Hurricane
6. Dust devil
7. Polar vortex
8. Thermometer
9. Horizon
10. Hail

Flight Science

Covering the science behind flight and aviation.

1. I'm a machine that can fly high in the sky; with wings and engines, I soar and glide.
What am I?

2. I'm the force that opposes gravity, helping birds and planes stay in the air, I'm a necessity.
What am I?

3. I'm a flying machine with spinning blades, lifting off the ground, I'm quite the parade.
What am I?

Flight Science

4. I'm a man-made object that soars through the air with a pointed tip and fins; I'm quite debonair. What am I?

5. I'm a type of aircraft lighter than air, with a large envelope filled with gas, I float with flair. What am I?

6. I'm the force that slows objects down in flight; with air resistance and lag, I'm a powerful might. What am I?

7. I'm the angle at which a wing meets the air, affecting lift and drag, I'm a crucial affair. What am I?

Flight Science

8. I'm a flying machine that uses a large fan, hovering above the ground, I'm quite a sensation. What am I?

9. I'm a small, remote-controlled flying device used for fun or taking photos; I'm quite precise. What am I?

10. I'm the distance a plane can fly without stopping; from fuel to efficiency, I'm always hopping. What am I?

Flight Science

Fun Facts

The Wright brothers, Orville and Wilbur, were the first to achieve controlled, powered flight in 1903

Birds inspired many early flying machines, including Leonardo da Vinci's ornithopter designs.

Answer Key

1. Airplane
2. Lift
3. Helicopter
4. Rocket
5. Hot air balloon
6. Drag
7. Angle of attack
8. Hovercraft
9. Drone
10. Range

Silly Inventions and Gadgets

Highlighting unusual and amusing inventions and gadgets.

1. I'm an umbrella with a twist, keeping your head dry while your hands are free, I'm a quirky assist. What am I?

2. I'm a small device that keeps your chips fresh; with a snap and a pop, I prevent a snack mess. What am I?

3. I'm a gadget that cools in a flash, spinning ice cubes around, I'm quite a splash. What am I?

Silly Inventions and Gadgets

4. I'm a utensil that combines two utensils in one; I'm ready for food fun. What am I?

5. I'm a device that turns your stairs into a slope, I'm quite a dope. What am I?

6. I'm a cushion that covers your face with a built-in tube; I'm quite unnecessary dude. What am I?

7. I'm a machine that throws snacks in the air; with a catch and a chomp, I'm a dog's best affair. What am I?

Silly Inventions and Gadgets

Did You Know: The first patent for a snow globe was granted in Austria in 1900.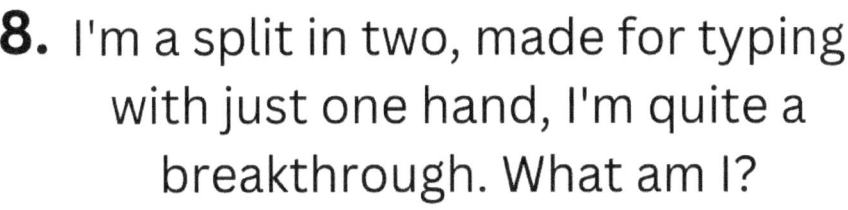

8. I'm a split in two, made for typing with just one hand, I'm quite a breakthrough. What am I?

9. I'm an object that writes made in the air; with printing technology, I'm a creative affair. What am I?

10. I'm a device that helps you see close, I magnify tiny things, and I'm a scientific trope. What am I?

Silly Inventions and Gadgets

Fun Facts

The Snuggie, a wearable blanket, has sold millions of units since its introduction in 2008

The Slinky, a popular toy, was invented by accident in 1943.

The fidget spinner was originally designed to help people with ADHD and anxiety.

Answer Key

1. Umbrella hat
2. Chip bag clip
3. Instant drink chiller
4. Spork
5. Stair slide
6. Snorkel pillow
7. Dog treat launcher
8. One-handed keyboard
9. 3D printing pen
10. Smartphone microscope attachment

Wacky Weather Phenomena

Exploring unusual and unexpected weather events and phenomena.

1. I'm a rare weather event where frogs or fish rain from the sky, scooped up by strong winds; I'm quite a surprise. What am I?

2. I'm a phenomenon where a river runs red due to algae blooms or minerals; I'm a sight to be tread. What am I?

3. I'm a ball of light that appears during a storm, often mistaken for UFO, I'm an electric form. What am I?

Wacky Weather Phenomena

4. I'm a bright and colorful light show in the polar sky, with dancing ribbons of green and red, I'm quite spry. What am I?

5. I'm a pillar of light that shoots up from the ground, I'm a natural phenomenon to be found. What am I?

6. I'm a strange weather event where it seems to rain spiders, carried by the wind, I'm an eight-legged glider. What am I?

7. I'm a rare weather event with stones of ice falling from the sky, often in the desert, I'm a sight to catch your eye. What am I?

Wacky Weather Phenomena

Did You Know: A waterspout is a tornado that forms over water.

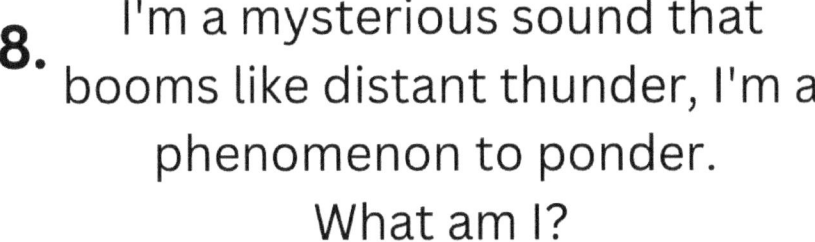

8. I'm a mysterious sound that booms like distant thunder, I'm a phenomenon to ponder.
What am I?

9. I'm a rainbow that's circular and appears around the sun, with colors swirling, I'm a beautiful phenomenon. What am I?

10. I'm a whirlwind made of flames, a fiery twister that's quite hot; during fires or volcanic eruptions, I'm often caught.
What am I?

Wacky Weather Phenomena

Fun Facts

A "fire rainbow" is a rare phenomenon caused by sunlight refracting through ice crystals in high-altitude clouds.

"Thundersnow" is a rare winter weather event where snow falls instead of rain during a thunderstorm.

Answer Key

1. Animal rain
2. Red tide
3. Ball lightning
4. Northern Lights
5. Light pillar
6. Spider rain
7. Ice fall
8. Skyquakes
9. Sun halo
10. Fire tornado

Strange and Unusual Animals

Covering a wide variety of animals with unusual or unique characteristics.

1. I'm a fish with a transparent head, deep in the ocean, I look quite bizarre, it must be said. What am I?

2. I'm a mammal that lays eggs and has a duck-like bill, with venomous spurs, I'm a quirky thrill. What am I?

3. I'm a bird with a huge beak and colorful feathers, I can mimic sounds, and I'm clever. What am I?

Strange and Unusual Animals

4. I'm a creature with blue blood and eight arms, living in the deep sea; I have many charms.
What am I?

5. I'm a reptile with a long neck and a shell, I can live for over a century, and I'm doing quite well. What am I?

6. I'm a mammal with a long snout and a scaly tail, I eat insects and live in the water, without fail.
What am I?

7. I'm a frog with transparent skin, you can see my organs, I'm a wonder of nature, a sight to be seen. What am I?

Strange and Unusual Animals

Did You Know: The axolotl, a salamander, can regenerate lost limbs and even parts of its brain.

8. I'm a bird with a spoon-shaped bill, wading in the water, I'm quite the colorful thrill. What am I?

9. I'm a creature quite bizarre, with a nose that's like a star. My tongue's a straw, so long and thin I slurp my meal from afar.

10. I'm a mammal with a long, sticky tongue, eating ants and termites, I'm always on the run. What am I?

Strange and Unusual Animals

Fun Facts

The blobfish, which lives deep in the ocean, has a gelatinous body that helps it withstand high water pressure.

The aye-aye, a type of lemur, has a long, thin middle finger that it uses to tap on tree bark to find insects.

Answer Key

1. Barreleye fish
2. Platypus
3. Kea parrot
4. Pacific octopus
5. Galapagos tortoise
6. Desman
7. Glass frog
8. Spoonbill
9. Aardvark
10. Anteater

Plants and Botany

Explores the fascinating world of plants, their diverse forms.

1. With leaves so green and a trunk so stout, I provide shade and oxygen; there's no doubt.
What am I?

2. I'm a plant that's small, with leaves so tiny and round, living on rocks or trees, sometimes close to the ground. What am I?

3. I climb and twist, reaching for the sky, with flowers and fruits, I'm quite spry. What am I?

Plants and Botany

4. Colorful and bright, I bring delight, attracting bees and butterflies with my sight.
What am I?

5. I'm a plant that grows in water, providing a home for fish, a lovely green, underwater dish.
What am I?

6. With needle-like leaves and a cone for a hat, I stand tall, an evergreen chap. What am I?

7. Tall and golden, swaying in the breeze, I'm a field of sunshine, that you'll surely seize.
What am I?

Plants and Botany

Did You Know: Bamboo, which is a type of grass, is one of the fastest-growing plants on Earth.

8. With juicy, red fruits hanging from my vine, I'm a summertime favorite, so sweet and divine. What am I?

9. I'm a plant that grows in the desert, storing water in my leaves, with spines to protect, I stand tall, defying the heat. What am I?

10. With leaves shaped like lobes, I stand tall and bold, my colors change from green to red, orange, and gold. What am I?

Plants and Botany

Fun Facts

The world's tallest tree is a coast redwood named Hyperion, found in California, USA. It stands at a staggering 379.7 feet.

Some plants, like the Venus flytrap and the pitcher plant, are carnivorous and can catch and digest insects to obtain nutrients.

Answer Key

1. A Tree
2. A Moss
3. A Vine
4. A Flower
5. An Aquatic Plant
6. A Pine Tree
7. A Wheat Field
8. Strawberry
9. A Cactus
10. A Oak Tree

Ecosystems

Explores the diverse and fascinating habitats found around the world.

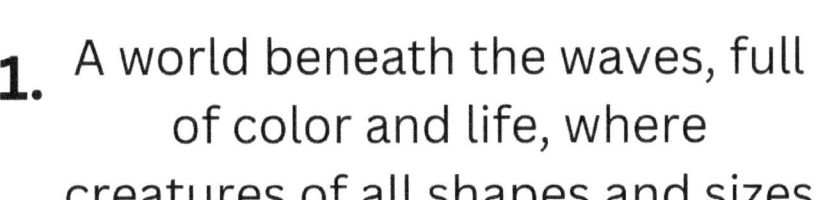

1. A world beneath the waves, full of color and life, where creatures of all shapes and sizes thrive. What am I?

2. Vast, dry, and sandy, home to cacti and camels, I'm where water is rare and precious. What am I?

3. Dense and humid, with tall trees and diverse creatures, I'm where water is plenty, and life abounds. What am I?

Ecosystems

4. Cold and icy, with penguins and polar bears, I'm found at Earth's ends, where the wind blows strong. What am I?

5. Between land and sea, where tides rise and fall, I'm a mysterious world of mangroves and mud. What am I?

6. Vast, open spaces with tall grasses and roaming herds, I'm a place where many animals find their homes. What am I?

7. Towering trees and dappled sunlight, I'm home to a parade of animals and birds that take flight. What am I?

Ecosystems

8. Up high in the mountains, where the air is thin, I'm a rocky haven for plants and animals to fit in. What am I?

9. A wetland teeming with life, where water and land unite, I'm home to nesting birds and frogs that sing at night. What am I?

10. Unique and found on certain shores, where the ocean meets land, I'm a place of rock pools and crashing waves. What am I?

Ecosystems

Fun Facts

Rainforests cover only about 6% of Earth's surface but are home to more than half of the world's plant and animal species.

Wetlands, such as swamps and marshes, act as natural water filters, absorbing pollutants and helping to maintain water quality in nearby rivers and streams.

Answer Key

1. Coral Reef
2. Desert
3. Rainforest
4. Polar Region
5. Tidal Marsh
6. Grassland
7. Forest
8. Alpine Ecosystem
9. Swamp
10. Rocky Zone

THANK YOU

AS AN INDEPENDENT PUBLISHER

We rely on you.

Please let us know if we can make your experience even better. We respect constructive criticism as it allows us to keep getting better. If you have any issues, message us online!

Please consider leaving us a review on Amazon!

Wonderfully Wacky

SCIENCE RIDDLES

For Curious Kids

www.ingramcontent.com/pod-product-compliance
Lightning Source LLC
Chambersburg PA
CBHW071011120726
47910CB00004B/1471